Because you are incomparable

you can do everything

Fascinating stories

about our limitless potential and the infinite strength within us

Table of content

It does not matter what others say 3

The way to school 13

My new friend.................27

In the nearby garden.................37

The magic stone 49

Olli and the rattlesnake gang 58

Unity is strength.................71

It does not matter what others say

"What would you like to become when you will grow up?" Asks Mara to her friends.

She is sitting on a bench near the playground having a picnic with her three friends Nele, Emma, Olivia and her cousin Luca.

Today the weather is nice, unlike other days, so the group decided to go out and enjoy it together.

Luca shrugs his shoulders as he takes a sausage sandwich from his packed lunch.

"I don't know yet". He bites his sandwich angrily. " Sometimes I think to myself that I want to become a doctor. Then a week later I want to be a firefighter, then an architect.

I even thought about being a pilot. I'm really undecided". He is always very honest with his friends.

Emma's smile fills her face, causing her red cheeks to almost fade in front of her little eyes. " Well, I already know exactly what I want to become," she says with excitement and bright eyes. "My dad works at the riding school at the city's suburb. I always have

the permission to go there during the holidays, and from the first time I was there, it was clear to me that I wanted to become the manager and a riding coach of the ranch".

Nele nods to her friend quickly, because she knows how much Emma loves horses. She takes a sip of her homemade lemonade and wipes her mouth with the back of her hand:

"I will follow in my mother's footsteps and one day take over her flower-boutique," she proudly announces.

"That's for sure," the other children respond unanimously, while a flock of birds fly above them, trilling a small song with a loud chirp.

"And you, Olivia?" asked Mara, waiting anxiously for an answer. The quiet girl first looks closely at her friends with wide eyes, then smiles and puts aside her bread. She slowly moves one of her long locks of hair from her face, and she says: "I want to become a teacher "she says quietly, taking her sandwich again and biting it. " I want to teach to children. I think I would like it".

Mara smiles back and nods politely. Even though she cannot imagine Olivia as a teacher right now, she still knows she will be able to have her own path and one day she is going to be a wonderful teacher. Everyone knows that she lacks self-confidence and that she always finds it very difficult to present something in front of the class. When that happens, the day before she is always very excited and can barely sleep. She knew she could work on it and train herself to manage her emotions, so nothing would stand in her way in the future.

Mara was pretty sure. To be honest, when she was in front of the whole class and everyone was waiting for her to say something, she always had a feeling of sinking into his stomach.

It was not even the worst thing: she had to show everyone her work, and if it was not good enough and the whole class would notice. So, she understood Olivia very well.

Luca laughs softly. "To become a teacher, you have to work a little more on your self-esteem," she tells Olivia out of the blue.

"Luca", Nele warned him, and at this point he lowers his head and pretends to have said nothing.

"I know that too, Luca," Olivia responds in a resolute tone. But in her eyes Mara can read that she has been offended in some way by that statement. Olivia tightens her lips and lowers her head. Unfortunately, he has no words to defend himself.

So, Mara takes over. "Everything will come", she says, addressing to Luca. "After all, we are still young, and we have time to work on ourselves".

At this point, she smiles at Olivia and her friend smiled back and thanks her for her help silently. We all know that you are not a person who is inclined to give a speech in front of many people, but you know more than anyone how it feels like to do such thing. Luca raises his hands as a sign of resignation: "It's all right. It was just to say something.

As a teacher you have to speak in front of the whole class. And not only that. You have to communicate with parents and other teachers too", he lists it bluntly.

Olivia nods. "I know all this and I am sure I will be able to handle it" "I think so too" Emma answers back with agreement by hitting her shoulder with her elbow.

"What about you, Mara?" Asks Nele while untying her braids from her long blond hair to braid it tighter again. "What do you want to do when you grow up?".

Yes, now it was her turn. But Mara did not really know whether to tell her friends about her career aspirations. At the last family celebration, held over the weekend, her uncle asked her what she wishes to become in the future.

Mara was full of expectations and when she said it out loud, her cousin immediately burst out laughing. She wanted to tell her that women were not fit for that profession and that she should choose something else to do.

But Mara was convinced, she did not want to choose anything

else. She wanted to know what her friends wished to do when they grew up, but she did not expect them to ask her what she wanted to become.

For an instant, she regretted asking that question. The anxiety increased, and Mara is fearing her friends' reaction.

She almost thinks of saying another profession, so her friends do not make fun of her. Not a second after, she reconsidered her thoughts. Why should not she say out loud her dream job? After all, her life and her future were at stake, and no one had the right to comment on that except herself.

Mara needed a lot of courage to reveal that to her friends. With a deep breath, she stares at her cousin's and her friends' face that are waiting for her to answer. She braids her fingers, clears her throat and she says: " When I grow up, I want to become a policewoman" she announced with a cautious but determined voice. Everyone remained silent and Mara felt the restlessness rise again inside of her. The silence was penetrating, in the adjacent park you could hear the sounds of the city in the background.

Mara swallows loudly as her cousin and friends stare at her with frowning eyebrows.

"I want to help people and catch criminals". "Maybe I can also help them find the right path. Anyways, I guess this is a pretty exciting and interesting job".

"Do you want to become a policewoman?" asked Olivia. " And chase the criminals?"

Mara nods. "Yes, it's the job I want to do when I grow up".

Luca shakes his head. "I don't know, Mara", he replies, looking at her with his eyebrows raised. "I don't know if it is a job that would suit you"

Mara writhes her face like she does not understand his statement. But in reality, she understands it perfectly, and she realises that Luca has the same preconceptions as her cousin. " Why should not it be something for me?" she asks while anger is rising inside of her. Not only anger but even determination. The determination she needed to defend her dreams.

Luke understands from the tone of Mara's voice that she was not very enthusiastic about his statement. "Well, you're a..."

"Girl" completes her sentence.

He nods. "Yes, exactly. Maybe it's a men's job".

Emma puts away her packed lunch. " Well, I'm not so sure that this is a job that suits women, I happen to see only male cops".

Luke smiles victoriously.

"I don't agree," says Nele. "On TV, I always see policewomen, and I think they do their job very well". Disappointed by Luca and Emma, Mara has nevertheless listened and accepted without commenting their career choices, instead of trying to dissuade them.

At that moment, she wanted to tell him that she did not care what they thought, and that she would definitely become a cop. But after all, she was in front of his friends, and she did not want to lose them over such arguments.

She shrugs and smiles. " Well, maybe Luca will change his mind again in a few weeks," she says. "It's getting dark," she says. " We should start packing our bags and go home". She knows that the way she is handling the situation right now is not good for her confidence, but in that case, she knew it was the best thing to do. On the way home, the children talk about completely different things. About the houses' colours, the cars that are passing by, the time and about school.

Once they reach the crossroad, they go separate ways. Luca and Emma take the left was, and Nele and Olivia the right way. Mara was the only one to keep walking straight.

After saying goodbye, Mara walks home alone. Still sad about the fact that his friends do not approve of his career choice, she slows down and walks with her head down. The sun slowly sets behind the houses, giving way to the moon and the stars. She has to hurry, because she promised her parents that she would be home before evening.

Why does everyone say that police work is not suitable for women? Yet so many women work there. In reality, we live in an age in which these things should not count at all. Moreover, Mara has already done more than one research on this profession and nowhere she has found that women were not requested as police officers.

It was necessary to have good grades and a good degree to work there.

She already had good grades, and in the future, she would also get a good degree. After all, she was only nine years old and many things could have changed in her school career.

In order to do that, she had to be good at sports, show empathy and be able to act rapidly.

It would not be easy, but Mara was well aware of it.

As she turns into the yard, her mother immediately catches her eye. She was kneeling in the garden in front of the house looking after the flowers. "Hello mom", she greets by raising her hand. Her mother turns to her and stands up. "Hello Mara, my dear. You arrived just in time, dinner is almost ready". She wipes her forehead with the back of her hand and blows a lock of hair from her face.

Mara nods. "All right," she says with melancholy as she climbs the four steps leading to the front door.

However, her mother notices that something is wrong with her daughter immediately.

"What's wrong?" she asks with concern in her voice. " Didn't you have a good day? Did you argue with somebody?"

Mara stops and puffs out loud. Actually, she wanted to sort it out with herself, by thinking about it a little more and forgetting about it later. She did not want her parents to care about her problems. But unfortunately, in her pain, she has forgotten to make a happy face in front of her mother. At this point, she should have told her what happened.

Discouraged, she takes off her backpack and sits on the stairs. In not even a blink of an eye, her mother sits next to her. " Hey, what's wrong?" she asks again, stroking her back. "Tell me".

Mara snorts again. "We were at the playground, and I asked my friends what they wanted to do when they will grow up".

Her mother squeezes her lips and struggles to smile as tears form in Mara's eyes. She clearly remembered the last family celebration, because it was she who defended and comforted her daughter.

"Then, I told her that I wanted to become a policewoman", continues Mara. "Olivia said nothing, Nele was on my side, but Luca and Emma said that it is not a job for women". Her voice trembles with anger and pain as she struggles to not to cry.

Her mother smiles affectionately as the streetlights light up around her. "Oh, Mara," she says, "I know it's hard. But stay true to what you like and what you want to do. You do not have to worry about what others say, but you have to learn to deal with the fact that everyone has their own opinion about certain things. Some people express their opinions out loud in the hope of changing other people's minds, and others keep their opinions to themselves because they do not want the other person to feel offended.

People are very different and it is good: Everyone is unique and special!

You are too. You will find out in your lifetime. In any case, do not let yourself get down. If you want to become a police officer, then do everything to become one. Your father and I will support you in every way possible".

Her mother's words struck her.

It seemed that they had come right from her heart and they triggered something in her.

Mara suddenly felt freed, relieved and understood. Realising that keeping everything inside is not good for the soul, she understood that it was a relief to talk about their worries and fears, and that it was not wrong to ask for help from time to time. Mara smiles relieved and hugs her mother. "Thank you, mom, I will try to believe in myself and in my dreams". Mara wanted to reassure her mom, and she finally really believed in herself.

It was very important to do so, for her growth and future.

She has to accept that her cousin, Luca and Emma were not enthusiastic about her career aspirations, but she did not have to let that stand in her way, because if otherwise, she would become an unhappy person, and that she promised herself to never let that happen.

It's your turn

What did you like most about this story?

_____
_____
_____
_____
_____
_____
_____
_____
_____
_____
_____
_____
_____
_____

It's your turn

What did you learn from this story?

_____

_____

_____

_____

_____

_____

_____

_____

_____

_____

_____

_____

_____

_____

The way to school

Kindergarten was great, but Benjamin was looking forward to finally going to school. He had a very nice teacher. On the first day of the school, Mrs. Meyer warmly welcomed him and many of his kindergarten friends, and Benjamin had received a large backpack.

He had a very nice teacher. On the first day of school, Mrs. Meyer warmly welcomed him and many of his kindergarten friends, and Benjamin had received a large school backpack containing many treats and useful things such as sharpeners, erasers, notebooks, and pencils, which he would use at school.

There was a watch in the backpack.

Benjamin already knew how to read the clock, he learned how to do it in kindergarten, so he always knew what time it was.

While the first day of school is devoted to presentations, the second day represents the very beginning of classes. Benjamin could write his name and knew some letters, but his dream has always been to learn to read alone. Even though it was nice to be read by mom and dad, going to school meant that he would finally learn to read by himself.

It could have been all wonderful, only if...

If it wasn't for the ride to school...

The way to school scared Benjamin.

In front of his house, there is a busy street.

Of course, there was a pedestrian path and also a wide lane for bicycles, however, there were many noisy cars.

And Benjamin knew from kindergarten that even cars could be

dangerous.

"Children are often neglected by motorists," Raabe, the teacher, had often explained to them when they went on a trip with the group. " "A big car is fast, and unfortunately the driver often accelerates too much. So, you have to pay close attention", she had warned them over and over again.

He had seen what could happen, like when he had an accident with Johanna, the older sister of Paul, his kindergarten friend.

He'd been going to school for a long time now, and more precisely, he'd go there by riding his bike. A year earlier, unfortunately, she had been involved in an accident with a truck driver, while trying to turn right at a traffic light. The bicycle had become a pile of garbage and Johanna was also not well.

She had to go to the hospital, her right leg was broken, as well as some minor bruising. She had to stay in the hospital for a long time and then she had her leg plastered for several months. Benjamin had gone to visit her in the hospital with Paul, and she was very happy with the visit. Smiling, she explained then that she was lucky that nothing worse had happened.

Benjamin looked at her and said, "Well, what happened to you seems pretty bad".

He would rather not be hit by a car or even a truck.

Unfortunately, it was that intersection where Johanna had had the accident, that Benjamin had to cross to go to school.

Although they had installed a mirror, so that the truck drivers had a better view of the bike path, this did not change the bad feeling that Benjamin felt at that intersection, even if he always respected the traffic light.

He was always waiting for the green to go off, checking again to make sure the cars stopped, and only then did he cross the street quickly.

Benjamin had done it many times, but each time he was under his parent's surveillance.

He had never crossed the road alone, there was always a hand holding him. Tomorrow, however, he would have had to cross the street alone, without a hand to hold him, and without an adult to watch over him.

After that, his way to school took him across the city park. At least there were no cars here. Benjamin had to cross a lake with some swans. Uncle Herbert once told him that when he fed ducks, he had to watch out for swans, because they could bite and the blows they gave with their wings caused bruises.

Benjamin didn't know if it was true, but he was a little scared at the thought of it.

And tomorrow, yes, he would have had to walk that long road alone.

"And don't waste time," said his mother. "Or you'll be late for school".

No, he didn't want to be late. But what would have happened if the shoe would have been untied? Benjamin knew how to tie his shoes, but sometimes he couldn't do it right, and then he had to start all over again, and with a big backpack on his back, it certainly wouldn't have been easier.

Benjamin was very concerned about what would happen if he arrived late.

What if they learned to read exactly when he was late? He would have been the only first-class student who couldn't read.

No. He didn't want to be late.

The watch on his wrist was ticking, it would help him not to be late. The best thing for him was to still run in front of the lake, and even to the playground.

The playground where he loves to go with his mom and dad. The playground where he liked to meet his friends and build sandcastles, or play climbing the mountain. The playground was great.

But that morning, when he passed the playground with Mom and Dad, it didn't seem as fun as usual. It was lonely and felt abandoned, and Benjamin didn't even want to imagine what or who was hiding in the dark shadows. But it wasn't a problem, with Mom on his side. Tomorrow, however, he would have to cross that way all by himself.

There was no hand to hold to give him courage and confidence And then there was the bakery.

Of course, he wasn't afraid of the bakery. On the contrary, he liked to go to the bakery. The saleswoman is called Anna and always greeted him.

It smelled so good, and when his dad took him shopping, he would always buy him a little cake or chocolate while he got coffee.

But in the last few days, as he went to school with his parents in the morning, there was a big old dog tied up outside the bakery. His master was sitting inside, drinking coffee with him and reading a newspaper. When they approached, the dog stood up and growled menacingly. Benjamin grabbed his father's hand and pulled it to himself quickly.

Even though the dog was tied up, there was something very threatening about him. Benjamin was very pleased when they left the dog at a safe distance behind them.

What if he walked past the bakery alone tomorrow and the dog would still be there? What if he got free and chased him somewhere? Somewhere far from his way to school! Away from school! What if he's lost?

Or worse still, if the dog had caught him? What would have done to him, such a big and dangerous dog?

The stick he carried with him

each time he was outside, was like a real grandmother to him.

Benjamin was very fond of being with Grandma Gerda: he was happy that she was the one opening the door when he heard her warm and familiar voice.

"How long have you been sitting there?" Grandma Gerda asked.

Benjamin didn't know exactly how long he had been sitting on the stairs. He was looking at his watch. The hour hand marked three, and the minute hand was just before twelve. So, it was almost three. But how long has he been sitting there?

"Well, you come in first, little man", Grandma Gerda convinces him cheerfully. "It is not good to sit on the cold stairs".

Benjamin notices how cold it was in the stairwell. The invitation comes at the right time.

"Yes, all right, grandma," replies Benjamin, relieved, getting up to jump the few steps.

Together, the two enter Grandma Gerda's cosy apartment.

"Sit down, my boy", invite him. " Do you want some tea?"

Benjamin accepts without hesitation. Grandmother Gerda's teas were legendary because she dried fruits and herbs and prepared her tea blends herself.

"Yes, please!" he replies cheerfully.

Granny Gerda put on the fire the tea kettle from the bright paint. Then he took from the shelf an old, bulbous porcelain teapot with a floral pattern and poured some from one of his cans into a tea strainer, which he hung in the teapot.

While the two waited for the tea kettle to blow its whistle,

Grandma Gerda took more of her delicious cookies from the cupboard. Benjamin took one right away.

"Delicious as always. Thank you very much," she says with a full mouth, making Grandma Gerda smile.

"What's going on?" asks Grandma Gerda, who noticed something was amiss.

"Tomorrow, I have to go to school alone for the first time," Benjamin confesses in a low voice, happy to finally talk to someone about his matter.

"Yes, but aren't you excited to go to school?!, Benjamin," replies Grandma Gerda, a little surprised.

"Of course, I'm looking forward to school. But the road scares me, and there were so many things that could happen," Benjamin sighed.

The kettle whistled and Grandma Gerda got up to pour the tea. The smell of herbs and fruit filled the room.

"Hmmm", Grandma Gerda grumbles, now facing Benjamin again, "do you still know the way to school?".

"Of course, I do!" replies Benjamin. "I've already done it a few times with Mom and Dad".

"And something ever happened?" asked grandma Gerda.

"No, but there was always someone looking after me," Benjamin admits quietly.

Grandma Gerda thought about it, tapping her foot on the floor. She took a biscuit and crunched it thoughtfully.

Benjamin looked at her hopefully, he knew she had an answer to his issue. Surely, she could help him.

"Maybe you could go with Silke". Silke lives in the same building as Benjamin, just an apartment below them. Silke attended her class, they had the same path, so he could go to school with her. Silke was an older girl than Benjamin. How could she have asked if she wanted to go to school with him?

What would you think of him? Would you laugh at him when he told you he was afraid to make it to school? Would you have told the others?

Grandma Gerda poured steaming tea on both of them and the delicious smell drove away Benjamin's worries for a moment. He dipped a cookie in the cup and put it in his mouth.

"That's good," he mutters with his mouth full.

"With a biscuit in my stomach, I will see the world differently," Benjamin says cheerfully as he took a satisfying sip of the wonderfully scented tea.

"I think I'll go to Silke and ask her. Thanks for the tip, see you soon and thanks for the tea and cookies." Benjamin is happy, and he's already out the door bouncing down the stairs.

In front of Silke's door, he concentrated on not losing his courage again. He took a deep breath and pressed the bell button.

Benjamin heard the ringing of the bell. But nothing happened. He waited, he pressed the button again, but nobody answered.

"There is no one in the house," Benjamin thinks with disappointment and slowly began to walk up the stairs of the building.

He went straight to his room. His wristwatch indicated that he was close to 6:00 p.m.

His mom told him that he should take a bath first, have dinner and then go to bed early.

He should have been well rested to better face the school of the following day.

Benjamin took his squeaky duck and went into the bathtub. He put on his favorite CD and Mom opened the faucet and ran the water. He added some bath salts to the water and a refreshing scent of lavender and mandarin filled the room. With him, as always, there was his duck.

Mom folded the dryer towels and put them on the shelf.
"Mom, can you come to school with me tomorrow?" Benjamin asks hesitantly.
Mom put aside the towel she had just collected and leaned over to him. Stroking his hair, he asks him, "Is that why you've been so quiet all day? School? Is someone bothering you?" asks Mom.
"But no," Benjamin replies. "Everything is fine at school. It's the way to school, Mom. Can you come with me, please?"
"Oh, my dear, I would love to. But you know I have to get back to work tomorrow. You know the way. I am sure that nothing will happen to you", Mom answers by stroking his hair one last time, "you are already grown up. You can do it yourself".
Benjamin was aware that he was already great. He was just uncertain if he could make it to school. He let himself sink into the hot water and Mom washed his hair. After drying, he put on his pyjamas and Mom dried his hair.
The dinner was quiet. Benjamin lazily chewed his bread, his parents talked about the groceries that his dad would have to do the next day after work.
After dinner, while Benjamin was brushing his teeth, his father came in. With a toothbrush and a lot of

foam in his mouth, Benjamin asks him: "Dad, can you put me to bed tonight?".

"I'd love to, honey," he says. "Do you want to choose the bedtime story or should I tell you one?".

"Oh, I'd like you to choose Dad," replies Benjamin, brushing his teeth. Dad left the bathroom to pick out a story to read that night.

Benjamin also prepared quickly. He had just crawled under the cozy blanket. When his dad came into the room with a new book. He sat in the chair next to Benjamin's bed and started reading "Kiki Cat goes to school". There were beautiful images on every page, sometimes something to compose like a puzzle or coloring. That evening he could no longer color, but Benjamin was looking forward to taking the pencils in the coming days.

"Dad, can't you come to school with me tomorrow?" Benjamin suddenly asks. Dad seemed amazed. " But Benjamin. I have to go to work tomorrow. What will my boss think if I don't arrive on time?".

"I only ask because tomorrow I have to go to school alone and there is no one to take care of me and can carry me there".

"Nobody? Who says that?". The two parents had already discussed the problem. After all, for a child to go to school alone was a big step. As a result, he had already achieved something.

He pulled out of his pants pocket a small cloth figurine by Kiki Cat. There was a small chain with a clasp on the figurine so that it could be attached to the school backpack or trouser pocket. " Here, this is Kiki Cat. She will be with you and take care of you". Benjamin took the figure and imagined it growing and taking it by the hand. Of course, he knew the statue wasn't real, but he still felt that holding it in his hand made him feel a little better than without it. Also, he liked Kiki Cat. And a good luck charm is never wrong.

That night, Benjamin fell asleep with Kiki Cat in his arms, while his father was reading the story.

In the morning, the rays of the sun shining through his window woke him up before his mother. Kiki Cat was lying next to him. It seemed to give him an encouraging look as if to say: "Get up and say goodbye to the day". You can do it!"

Benjamin dressed in a flash and rushed to the breakfast table. Mom looked up from her coffee and was amazed.

"Are you up?" he asks.

His father, who was putting the slices of bread in the toaster, adds: "Well, did you sleep well?".

"And how," replies Benjamin, radiant. His hand checked his trouser pocket to see if Kiki Cat was also in his pocket. With her, he almost felt no longer anxious and knew that he would be able to go to school.

After breakfast, he quickly brushed his teeth, put on his jacket, and took his file. He was already in the stairwell and going on an adventure.

As he passed Silke's apartment, his steps slowed. Inside, everything was quiet through the small window above the door and no light shone. There seemed to be no one in the house. Somehow, he had hoped to go with Silke. His hand searched in his pocket and carefully squeezed the little Kiki Cat. Then he cheered himself up.

"I can do it," he says to himself as he walked down the stairs. When he opened the front door, however, he was very pleased.

Silke was in the courtyard. She was standing there, waiting for something.

"Tell me, would you like to go to school with me? I don't want to go alone," says Silke goodbye.

So, she was waiting for anybody, but him.

"Of course, we can go together," Benjamin responds with relief. All the worries had been swept away and together with Silke, the way to school was child's play.

They looked at the traffic lights together to make sure no cars ran the red light, and the swans didn't scare them anymore.

Together they would be able to deal with any dangerous swan. What about the shadows in the solitary playground? They also did not scare him anymore. In two, there was no need to fear the shadows anymore. Courage and trust came by themselves.

Together they would never be late for school, and if his shoe had untied, he would have simply put down his briefcase, and Silke could have watched him for a moment while he tied his shoe. As always. Nothing would go wrong.

Benjamin was so relieved that he immediately said: Yes, we will go together".

Together they walked along the noisy road to the intersection. The pedestrian lights turned green just as they were about to press the button. The cars stopped and neither left until the two reached the other side and the pedestrian light turned red again. Only when the traffic light turned green again did the cars leave.

It had worked before.

Now she was walking in the park with Silke. The swans didn't even approach him.

With Silke, he did not feel smaller, but bigger. Almost as big as Silke, although she was taller than him. Nevertheless, Benjamin's courage grew with every step and he seemed to be as tall as you.

He felt even taller, as tall as his dad. If he kept it up, he would have become a giant.

The shadows of the playground did not seem threatening at all, but on the contrary, they seemed to wish the two a good trip to school.

And the last obstacle, the dog on a leash in front of the bakery was suddenly small. Benjamin walked by and smiled at him. Just then, the dog stopped growling.

Now, the dog was not that big, and the road to school was a "piece of cake" that he could handle on his own. He didn't need Silke or Kiki Cat, but it was nice to have them as friends.

It's your turn

What did you like most about this story?

_____

_____

_____

_____

_____

_____

_____

_____

_____

_____

_____

_____

_____

_____

It's your turn

What did you learn from this story?

_____

_____

_____

_____

_____

_____

_____

_____

_____

_____

_____

_____

_____

_____

My new friend

The outdoor walls were dark, and some were rather shabby. The wood was rotten and probably, if touched with their finger, the whole building would collapse completely. The windows were broken, probably because they were smashed with stones. On one side, the roof had almost completely collapsed due to a broken branch. Before and after school, Tobias walked past this creepy old building every day. It made him a little sad that he was left to himself and that other people were hurting him, too. Why did people do these things? After all, they didn't own it. This old house once belonged to someone who cared for and loved it. People used to live there, and the house offered them protection and security. Now it was trampled on all sides and nobody cared how it looked. For as long as Tobias could remember that old house had been there, and every day, he saw more and more of it disappear from the scene. He had to admit that the house fascinated him a lot, and if he had the courage, he would have taken a look inside. But his charm was tempered by his fear because there was something very disturbing about that house. When the sky was gray and it was raining, it seemed even scarier. But today Tobias was lucky because the sun was shining. As he was coming home, he decided to stop just outside the house. The property was fenced with an old, rusty fence. A sign read: Do not enter! Parents were responsible for their children. This sign should have kept people and especially children away from the dilapidated building, but unfortunately not many respected it. A lot of kids had parties there, and the house was perfect for bravery tests. Months ago, his friends told him they wanted to come in after school, but fear had always kept them away. It was clear to

Tobias that he would never see the inside of the house. That sign was there for a reason, and anyone could see that entering that building was dangerous. The open door that directly opened the road to the front door creaked, as the wind moved it. Tobias winced with shock and took a step back. The only disturbing atmosphere, which prevailed even in the garden of the property prevented him from  entering, although the open door seems very inviting. There were days when it was completely lost in the view of the old building, and today was no exception. Every time he stopped to look at him, he found something new. Today, for example, he realizes that the terrace railing has collapsed. Yesterday it was not like that. Suddenly, Tobias hears a small sound. At first, he wonders if he heard it or if his ears were playing tricks. But as soon as his thought ends, he notices it again. "What is that?" he asks, without getting an answer. One thing was certain, this sound came from inside the house. The boy squints and leans his head forward a little, hoping to recognize something, but this also did not work. Here it is again! This time he was stronger and Tobias was almost out of breath when he realized it looked like a cat's caterwauling. Is there a cat trapped in the house? "Hello", he shouted in the direction of the house and took a step towards it. However, his conscience immediately warns him that in no case should he enter the property. He was torn and did not know what to do. If there had been a cat locked in the house, he would have. If there was a cat in the house, he might have needed his help, because he couldn't get out on his own. But how could he do that if he wasn't allowed in? Or if he didn't dare? Tobias took a deep breath and continued to listen, now the meowing was calmer again. There was something there, he was sure of it. A part of him told him that he was imagining it and that he shouldn't act accordingly, but a larger part of him said he had to get to the bottom of it, and that meant breaking the rules and entering the house, even though in the end it would turn out to be a big mistake. These words were easier to say than to do. Tobias was afraid of what was waiting for him inside. The boy was clear that he should put his fear deep in his mind and find his courage somewhere. There was no shame in being afraid, fear was even good, but it was simply an obstacle to some things. Again, he heard the meowing. "All right", he said, rubbing his hands. "I'll go in quickly, I'll get the cat and I'll get out quickly". That was his plan, and in his eyes, it sounds like a good plan. Once again he took a deep breath and took another step towards the property. But suddenly a fierce wind arose, so the garden door blew vigorously back and forth. Tobias jumped back, frightened. The tree next to it creaked, and he noticed something slamming against the windows from the inside, and the terrace railing collapsed completely. Tobias' fear took hold of him again. He turned and ran to his home. The old and disturbing house is located at the beginning of his property, so he only needs a short and quick sprint to enter his front yard. Without wasting time, he walks up the stairs, opens the front door, and closes it behind him. As soon as he had arrived within its four secure walls, he turns immediately and looks out the window. His heart is racing and his breath is fast. He wants to know if something is following him, but fortunately, nobody was there. Lucky! Tobias laughs and shakes his head. " I shouldn't think so much about the house," he says to himself by putting down his backpack and heading to the kitchen because it smells like delicious pancakes prepared by his mom. All night he couldn't forget what had happened the day before. He had a hard time falling asleep, because every time he closed his eyes, the house appeared to him. He couldn't even get that cat out of his head. He had struggled with himself all night but failed to make a proper decision. At the breakfast, he wants to tell the incident to his parents, but he does not have the courage, or rather, does not find the words. He knows what his parents think of the house, and he also knows very well that he was forbidden to enter the property, no matter if he was alone or with his friends. Tobias simply doesn't know what to do, so this morning he decides to take a completely different route to go to school, just so he doesn't have to pass by the house. But that wasn't a solution either, he realises in the very first lesson. With a slow look, he lets his eyes wander through the classroom. Each pupil carefully listens to the teacher. Except for him, because his thoughts are directed only to the cat and the house. It cannot go on like this. Tobias suddenly realizes that he has to deal with the matter and that he must not abandon the cat. He must help him, and he knows that he needs his help. He decides that after school he would return there. It wasn't over for him. The school day was very slow and boring. Nervously, he stays in his seat in class from lesson to lesson, counting the minutes until the bell rings. As soon as he hears it, he collects his things, throws his backpack on his shoulders, and quickly leaves the school grounds, without even saying goodbye to his friends. When he arrives home, he feels a little nauseous, because today the sky was not blue and clear, but rather gray and gloomy. Tobias, however, has a mission to accomplish, and with careful and crawling steps, he approaches the squeaky gate of the garden. When he arrives, he holds the handle tightly so that the terrifying noise stops at least for a few seconds. With trembling hands, he now holds the cold iron in his hands and stares at the old house. It cracks and creaks at every corner. "Is there anyone?" calls inside, focusing on whether or not I can hear the cat again. "Is there anyone?" he prays not to hear that sound anymore. He moves when he hears a soft meow between the crackling and the creaking. All of a sudden, all his doubts and fears disappear and he realizes that he would save this helpless cat from this old and decaying house. Determined, he takes his backpack off his back and leans it against the garden gate to keep it open. After all, he did not know what was waiting for him inside and whether he had to quickly escape. He could not be disturbed by a closed garden gate. Tobias takes a deep breath and rubs his hands. He feels the beads of sweat collecting on his forehead. At the moment he claims that he is not afraid, but that he is highly respected. Although: "Being afraid is fair and human," he repeats to himself. " You cannot let it take over you, but it always helps with being careful". He strikes a pose like he's facing the biggest battle of his life. He probably is, thinking to himself. A breath later, he enters the property and heads for the front door. To reach it, however, he still has to climb three rotten steps. Carefully, master them one after the other with flying colors. Arriving in front of the door, just a little push with your hand opens with a deafening creak. Tobias retracts his neck and looks around again to be on the safe side. He certainly does not want anyone to take it, so it was clear to him too that he should carry out this action as quickly as possible. The floor under his feet was rotten and yielded at every step. Weeds grew from the

31

walls and seemed to want to take over the house. Water dripping from the ceilings and Tobias feels like he has landed in a completely different world. On the right, a collapsed staircase leads to the first floor. Tobias hopes that the cat is not up there, because he has no idea how to get there. For now, he decides to search the ground floor. "Where are you?" he calls quietly in the rooms. He feels like everything in this house is shaking and about to collapse, so try to be as careful as possible. " Are you here somewhere?" When he arrives at the living room of the old house, he is surprised to find a broken sofa inside, and his eyes widen even more when he finds a small black cat on top of it. They were both surprised when they noticed each other. The cat meows and wants to escape, but Tobias immediately kneels and extends his hand. "Hey, stay there," he says calmly. " I just want to help you". The cat stops and stares at him with wide, green eyes. Tobias sees that the kitten is very insecure and does not know if he can trust him or not. "Come here", he keeps talking to him. "I'll get you out of here". The cat turns once in a circle, then timidly walks towards him. The closer he gets to him, the bigger his smile gets. His heart rears and he completely forgets where he is while the cat sniffs her hand with her soft nose. " It's all right. You mustn't be afraid of me". Hearing his voice, take another step back. "Don't be afraid". He lengthens even more and before he notices it, the kitten nestles on him, letting himself be pet. Tobias laughs, he's the happiest person in the world right now. However, this happiness does not last very long because he realizes again where he is. Without thinking further about whether the cat likes it or not, he simply takes it in his arms. " We get out of here", he says and to his amazement he lets him do everything without any objection. When he walks through the front door outside in safe freedom, he even begins to purr. Lovingly, he wraps the little cat in her jacket while outside it starts to rain slightly. Tobias didn't think about what he would do with the cat once he got out of there. It was clear to him from the beginning that he would take him home and take care of him. However, he had not considered that he would then have to tell his parents where he had found him. This was the task he had to face now. "Where did you get the cat?" asks his mother, after skeptically letting him into the house and letting him take care of the cat first. Now he was sitting on a soft blanket and happily drinking milk from a small bowl. Tobias hesitates, but also realizes that this would not help and that he had to tell his mother the truth. This also required a lot of courage on his part. "I found it in the old house at the beginning of our settlement". Stunned, his mother opens her mouth and looks at him with anger, but then her expression changes to one of love. " Tobias", he says in a stern but empathetic tone. " I thought we discussed that you shouldn't go into that dangerous house. It's only a matter of time before it collapses". Tobias intuitively nods. " Yes, I know, Mom. But every time I passed by, I could hear the cat. I couldn't leave it in there. It was just as dangerous for him too. What else was I supposed to do?" His mother smiles and briefly looks at the cat, who in the meantime had snuggled up in the blanket and was sleeping peacefully. " Next time something like this happens, please come to us. We will be happy to help you. I'm not too happy that you did it all on your own, but I'm also a little proud of you for not giving up on it," he replies, but then raises a warning finger. " Promise me that next time you'll ask your father or me for help. Okay?" Tobias was relieved. "All right, Mom". He sits on the floor with the cat, who he has already called Lucky, and strokes him. " What are we going to do about the kitten now?" "Hmm", his mother starts thinking and sits next to Tobias. "How about we make flyers and post them everywhere? I'll make a call to the animal shelter right away. Maybe someone will miss it". Sadly, Tobias looks at his mother. "What if no one misses him or no one wants him anymore?" His mother knows exactly where he wants to go. Very gently, she strokes Lucky's head. "Then we'll keep him, of course". Tobias was just waiting for these words. "Really?" he asks again, just to be sure. When his mother nods, he immediately hugs her with wide arms. "Thank you. Thank you, mom, I will take care of this kitten". His heart was bursting with joy, and he knew that he and Lucky would become good friends.

It's your turn

What did you like most about this story?

_____

_____

_____

_____

_____

_____

_____

_____

_____

_____

_____

_____

_____

It's your turn

What did you learn from this story?

_____
_____
_____
_____
_____
_____
_____
_____
_____
_____
_____
_____
_____
_____

In the nearby garden

Jonas likes to play in the garden, but he doesn't want to go out today, and there's a reason why. Jonas always plays alone in the garden. There were houses with gardens all over the street, but he was the only child and had no one else to play with. Last year there was Elias, he lived a street away, but he came to play from time to time. "Because we don't have a garden," Elias would say. And then the two played in the garden for hours. But last year Elias and his family moved to another city. Elias's mother had found a new job and they no longer lived in a rented apartment, but they had bought a house with a garden. "Why don't you come and see me sometime," Elias said while greeting him. "Yes, I will," Jonas replies sadly. He says goodbye to his friend and goes to the garden to play. But he never visited him because the city where they moved as far away, too far away to play there. And what would have changed? Elias was gone and he was never coming to play again. Jonas has been playing solo ever since. Alone in his garden. Jonas thinks it was a shame that Elias didn't come anymore, but he also liked being alone in the garden. Here he was allowed to grow his vegetables and flowers that he took good care of. "Good morning daisies", he greeted them every morning while refreshing them with water. "Good morning, dear chives," he says while watering them as well. "Good morning, dear sunflower". The sunflower was his pride and his joy, it was already almost as big as him. "...and good morning tomato" adds Jonas while he uses the rest of the water from the watering can to moisten the soil under the tomato. "Tomatoes don't like water on their leaves," was what his aunt Lilli said when she brought him the tomato seedlings, along with a canopy of tomatoes that had since remained on top of the much-grown tomato plant in her garden. "It makes their leaves sick," added her aunt. Since then, Jonas has made sure that the tomatoes always get enough water, but never on the leaves. The tomato plant thanked him with beautiful red tomatoes, and Jonas had already picked the first ones. But in addition to his garden corner, his garden also had other things to offer. For example, there is Cosmo, the neighbor's cat. Jonas likes to play with Cosmo. Cosmo belongs to the Smiths, but the high fence that surrounds their garden was not an obstacle. The kitten likes it wandering around the other gardens, he loves to lie in the sun and when he caresses his legs of Jonas, he immediately knows what he wants. Then comes the moment of cuddling, which means she wants to be pampered for a long time. Jonas likes Cosmo very much and the two spend many hours together. Even when it rains, Jonas likes to go out in the garden, then he puts on his rain gear and goes into his mud kitchen to get muddy. In his mud kitchen, he mixes mud smoothies and cooks sand cakes or other specialties. He once offered Cosmo a mud soup with leaf inlays, which he politely refused. He didn't want to go out today. He looked out the window to the empty house next to his garden. The house had been empty since old Mr. Burkant moved into the nursing home. It is one of the oldest houses on the street, much older than the house where Jonas lives with his parents. The dark half-timbered beams were lined with dark red clinker bricks and ivy grew on the wall of the house. At the top of the roof were gargoyles on every corner. When it rained, the water gleefully splashed from their mouths into the eaves below them. The house also has a small tower. It has many large windows on the first floor through which you can see shelves full of books. There's also an armchair where old Burkant used to sit.

In front of the house, there is a large old pear tree. In the fall, Mr. Burkant was carrying a basket full of pears. "For the little one," he said. Sometimes Jonas would sit with him on the bench under the pear tree and hear him read a story, but after the old man had to go to a nursing home, the beautiful house remained empty. The windows were no longer lit and there was no more smoke rising from the chimney. It seemed that all life had disappeared from the walls with old Mr. Burkant. "Don't you want to go out?" his mother asks, but Jonas only shakes his head. Something was moving out there, the house next door wasn't empty anymore. A family arrived yesterday, and today the moving vans were parked in front of the house and they were brought in furniture and boxes. He was supposed to be happy that a family was coming with kids, but he didn't know them, and that worried him a little bit. Maybe they'd make new friends here. Maybe they would play together every day. But... what if they didn't? What if they turned him down? What if they weren't loving, but mean children? Like Robert, whom his mother invited six months ago. Robert... Jonas felt a shiver down his spine just thinking about him. Robert's mother and his mother had met at Pilates. They had the idea to let the kids play together. They had agreed accordingly to meet for coffee. Robert didn't like the garden, and Jonas didn't like Robert. This was clear from the very beginning. "Where's your PlayStation?" was Robert's greeting. "I don't have one. My parents think this kind of game makes you stupid," Jonas replied, whereupon Robert commented frowning. "So what do you do alone all day?" Robert asked. "I'm

going to my garden," Jonas replied proudly. "Come, I'll show you". Robert followed Jonas into the garden, in a bad mood. This was certainly not the beginning of a good afternoon. It was more of an introduction to a chapter of horror. At first, Robert sat bored on the swing. Then he started rocking higher and higher like a wild man. Jonas was afraid that his swing was going to break, but at one point Robert had suddenly jumped off the swing, directly into Jonas' garden. Like a madman, he had crushed three of the tomatoes then still very small. Since then, there's only one tomato left. Not one of the lettuce plants next to it had recovered. Jonas was paralyzed. With his mouth open and tears in his eyes, he stood in front of the remains of his beloved garden. Angered by the horror, he did not realize that the next disaster was already coming. "What do we have here?" Robert's voice echoed from the mud kitchen. Jonas had turned around. I wonder what Robert the Destroyer was up to now. It was then that Jonas saw Cosmo, slumbering unaware in the sun in his favorite place next to the mud kitchen. "A dirty cat," sounded ugly from the mud kitchen. Before Jonas could explain that Cosmo was an elegant and anything but dirty lady cat, the bucket of smoothie mud flew on the cat. The bucket barely missed Cosmo, but the smoothie had landed in her soft fur. The cat hissed angrily and disappeared over the fence with a leap without returning for more than a week. Jonas couldn't stand that rude Robert. "Mom!", screamed Jonas. "Your garden is no fun," Robert grumbled as he trotted past Jonas, kicked the bucket with the remnants of the mud smoothie so that it flew over the garden fence and landed directly on the Smiths' awning, leaving an unpleasant stain. Both mothers left the house. Robert complained to his mother about how boring it was to be there. Jonas turned to his mother with tears in his eyes. There was only one good thing about this visit. His mother wouldn't dare bring them back again. That was all that was buzzing in his head today. This experience had frightened him so much that he feared that the children next door would be just like Robert. He just wouldn't get rid of them again. They weren't visiting after all, but from now on they would live in this beautiful old house. What if they had blown his beloved Cosmo as much as Robert had? Would he still dare to go to his garden? And what about her poor plants? Would they jump on them, too? Of course, there is a border with Mr. Burkant's old house, but it consists of a hedge with holes just one meter high. When Mr. Burkant was still living in the old house, that didn't bother Jonas. On the contrary, it was often in the garden of the old man, where there was much to discover. He had once crawled into a bush and found an old forgotten pavilion inside. Here Jonas had found a small secret hiding place for himself. From time-to-time Cosmo the cat was in the pavilion to hunt mice. Old Mr. Burkant also had a pond in the garden, where depending on the season all kinds of animals could be observed. Jonas had found it interesting to observe tadpoles, for example, as they slowly transformed into frogs. Jonas always liked to go through one of the holes in the hedge with Cosmo to go exploring with her, but if the new kids didn't like her visits, what would happen? Jonas decides to do something about it, somehow, he has to find out something about these children. He then goes to the attic, where there are two small windows overlooking the facade of the neighboring house and from which he can see the truck parked in the driveway and the people bringing things into the house. Lying in front of the window, Jonas looks at what is happening in front of the neighbor's house and sees two children carrying something inside. "A boy and a girl, then..." says Jonas to himself when he sees them. "I think they're both my age. But I still have too little information, let's see what my mother knows". Jonas jumps the stairs to the ground floor where he meets his mother, who was sitting at the computer working. He didn't like to disturb Mom, but the uncertainty didn't give him peace. "Mom, tell me, do you know anything about the kids moving in next door?" "Only they're twins. Why don't you go introduce yourself? So, you can get to know each other right away", replies Mom without looking up from the screen. "Twins? It can't be," Jonas thinks. But Mom seemed too busy, so there was probably no point in asking her again. Maybe he'd have time for him later. Now he still didn't want to go to the neighbors. If the first meeting had been negative, I wonder if there had been a second chance. Jonas then goes to Dad's garage. Today was his day off. Normally he worked on computers in a large company, but in his spare time, he preferred to tinker with old machines. At the time he was disassembling an old bike, most of the time he could make it work. Sometimes he was helped by Uncle Horst. Today there was a lot of dirt, Dad had black stuff everywhere. On his hands, his face, his shirt, his pants... everywhere. "Tell me, Dad... do you know anything about the guys next door?" asks Jonas with caution. "I think I saw the two boys playing ball in front of the house. Why don't you go introduce yourself?" replies the father, already busy working on the bike again. Jonas was confused... two guys? That was clearly a girl... things were getting weirder and weirder, and going down there was now even more out of the question. There was something wrong. Jonas sits in his room and thinks. The window was open and the sun was shining outside. He wants to get out, but he can't get his new neighbor's kids out of his mind. From the window he sees the postman carrying two parcels to the Smiths. Jonas liked the mailman, he was always smiling, even when it was raining, and he often dedicated time to Jonas when he received mail. Jonas rushes to the door and waits for the mailman to arrive in the driveway. "Let's hope there's mail today," Jonas says quietly. But that's when the doorbell rings. "I'll take care of it!" she yells in the living room. "Thank you, honey," she plays her mother's voice, accompanied by the sound of her keyboard. Jonas opens the door and greets the postman with a "Hello Mr. Jansen, have you seen the neighborhood children?" Mr. Jansen smiles as usual and replies: "Yes, you haven't seen the two girls yet? Cosmo li has already said goodbye. The three seem to get along. Here's a package for your dad. Can you give it to him, please? And two letters to your mother". "Yes, thank you," Jonas replies abruptly and a bit confused. He takes the mail and with a "Goodbye, Mr. Jansen", Jonas greets and slowly closes the door. Two girls, then? This is getting weirder and weirder. He puts the letters next to Mom's computer. Mom was so absorbed in her work, she didn't even notice. Then Jonas brings the package to his father. "Put it on the workbench, honey," says Dad without looking up. " Surely those are the seals I've waited a long time for. They arrived at the right time". Dad wipes his hands with a cloth, but he doesn't clean them. He takes a knife and opens the package. "Have you been to the neighbors yet?" asked dad. "No, not yet. I don't want to," Jonas replies quietly. "Don't be afraid," Dad says. " You can't back out. Sooner or later, you will know each other". Dad looks in the package. "Oh, look. These were just the gaskets I needed to make the engine work again," explains Dad, radiant. She doesn't seem to notice Jonas leaving the room again, brooding. Back in his room, he closes the door and says to himself: "See you later, then". The new neighbors were starting to creep him out. Instead of getting answers, now his head was full of questions. Jonas throws himself on the bed, draws a book from his bookshelf, and browses it listlessly. He likes books. But at the moment his thoughts revolve only around the new family. How was he supposed to show up there? What was he supposed to say? What would have changed for him? Would everything has been better? Or worse? Who were those guys, anyway? Sometimes boys and sometimes girls and sometimes boy and girl... Jonas was confused. "It can't go on like this," Jonas thinks while putting the book back on his bookshelf. He gets up, sets his clothes, and decides to set the table for lunch. But first, he tells his father. "Dad, I'm setting the table," says Jonas, because he knows it's going to take him longer to wash off the fat. While he sets the table, his mother enters the room. "It's nice of you to set the table, honey. I'm sorry I had so little time for you before. But I still have to finish the paperwork for this afternoon". "Yes, I know," says Jonas. Mom always had time for him, only sometimes, when she had a lot to do with a project, she was very hasty. "I made fish sticks and potatoes with spinach," says Mom as she pulls the fish sticks out of the oven. She pours the spinach into a bowl and decorates it with a tablespoon of cream. "The way you like it best". "That's nice, Mom", Jonas was pleased. This was his favorite dish. His second favorite, right after pizza. But Mom knew how to make it his favorite. "Thank you," says Jonas and puts the potato bowl

on the table. Then Dad enters the room. He still has a black spot on his forehead. "It smells delicious," he exclaims while sniffing. When he tries to kiss Mom as she passes, she deftly avoids it and scolds him: "Go wash up first, you dirty boy. You can keep your fat to yourself," he says with a laugh, and Dad disappears again into the bathroom. Dad comes out of the bathroom and they all sit down, hold hands and recite a prayer together, just to end it with a: "Bon Appetit!" When all of them have something on their plate, and they appease the first hunger with a few bites, Dad asks again, "Have you already been to the neighbors?" "No," Jonas says quietly. "Why not?" Mom asks. Jonas was a little reluctant to answer and then says hesitantly, "I don't want to. I don't know what kind of people they are, if we get along or if it will be as terrible as it was with Robert". "Well, I hope it's another Robert". Dad frowns as he thinks about cleaning the tent by himself. "No, I don't think there will be a Robert like that ", says Mom. " But to find out who your new neighbors are, you won't be able to avoid meeting them. Honey, I understand that you have reservations about this, but look at it this way. Sooner or later, you will meet anyway. And it is better if you make the first move. The neighbor's kids are also strangers in the neighborhood, and they probably have similar concerns. But you already know how to move around and you can tell them something about the school and the neighborhood. I'm sure they will. I am sure they will be happy to hear you approach them". "Do you think?" Jonas was a bit skeptical, but somehow what Mom had told him made sense. He decides to go to the neighbors this week. Indeed, today, immediately after lunch Jonas gets up. "Stop. Don't you want some dessert?" asks dad. "No, not today." Jonas was too excited and a little afraid that his newfound courage would leave him again before reaching the neighbors. He quickly puts on his sneakers and rushes out. On the sidewalk, he slows down a bit. The neighbor's driveway was in front of him. The furniture carrier was long gone and now a minibus was parked outside the door. There was no sign of the children. As she approaches the door and is about to reach the doorbell, it opens and a girl sticks her head out the door. "Hi," says the girl. "I'm Isabel. And who are you?" Ugh, there's no Robert, Jonas thinks. "I'm Jonas," Jonas says hesitantly, reaching out his hand. "Hi, Jonas. I'm Max", sounds the voice of a boy. A boy his age pushes over the girl's head and grabs her hand to squeeze her tight. "So, you're not twins," Jonas stutters, still looking slightly overwhelmed. "My parents told me that twins had moved here." "Well ... Actually, there are four of us, to be exact", another head appears on the door and looks like the first. He tries to outdo the others, but he can't because Isabel wants to go through the door too. "Two boys and two girls," Max explains. "I'm glad you're here. I was starting to think there weren't any other children living here." "Not many. I'm the only one on the street ... Or rather, I was the only one," Jonas quickly improves. "Well, there are four of us now," Jonas quickly adds to himself. "Well, actually it was five counting Robert" improved Rosi. "ROBERT ???" Jonas had turned a little white at the tip of his nose while remembering "the horror visit". "Yes, my brother. You still have to meet him. But he's a little shy and he's still unpacking his plants to put in the garden," explains Max. "Plants, garden, shy," Jonas repeated in his mind and now he was pretty sure this Robert wasn't like his worst nightmare at all. The mystery about the neighborhood kids had cleared up and they seemed very nice. Over time, the five became best friends and Jonas was very happy that he was no longer the only kid on the street.

It's your turn

What did you like most about this story?

_____

_____

_____

_____

_____

_____

_____

_____

_____

_____

_____

_____

_____

It's your turn

What did you learn from this story?

_____

_____

_____

_____

_____

_____

_____

_____

_____

_____

_____

_____

_____

_____

_____

The magic stone

Marie walks, lost in her thoughts. Today she needs some time for herself, she needs to think and gather ideas, because on Friday her teacher, Mrs. Müller, announced that she has to present an essay at the end of next week. The mere thought of having to stand alone in front of the whole class and present her idea scares her. Marie is a rather quiet and reserved pupil, and when she sees her classmates determined and confident facing life, she must admit that she feels a bit of envy. She also wants to be like them, but in some situations, she just can't, so sometimes it happens that she gets angry with herself and wonders why she too can't be more carefree. After a loud sigh, she goes for a walk along the field behind her house. After a few steps through the garden, she arrives in the open field. Here she is allowed to walk alone because her parents can see  her from home. A cool autumn wind blows on her nose and a thin rain announces a gloomy day. After having breakfast together, she immediately went out. Mrs. Müller gave her the task of writing an essay about her life, perhaps about an exciting holiday. She could also have told a completely different story if she had wanted to. "Let your imagination run wild, Marie," said the teacher, smiling at her. Because Mrs. Müller knows very well that Marie is a very good writer, but she never wants to show it to everyone, and too many times she has been mocked by her classmates for this reason. There seems to be no room for special professions these days, thinks Marie. She was always very sure that one day she would be a writer, but it was from the third grade that almost all pupils made her understand what they thought of her writing, so she was no longer so sure of herself. The fact that she had already been mocked several times for her stories did not make it easier for her. At just the thought of it, Marie would feel sick to her stomach. Her heart throbs and she becomes very nervous. In her head, there are various scenarios about how to escape the lesson, but nobody seems to be the right one for her. After all, escaping, changing school, or pretending to be sick was not in her style. This decision would have postponed that moment, but it wouldn't have made her disappear from her life. She was aware that she could not escape. She looks up as a flock of birds leaves towards the south. She would have liked to be one of them. She would have been flying south with them, and she would return in the spring pretending that at this time no wise man was making her life difficult. Marie follows the swarm until she can't see it anymore, and then she proceeds on her way. However, something distracts her. She stops on her steps, frowns, and squeezes her eyes to see better. Just in front of her, in the ditch next to the path, something bright flashes. Marie is not sure, because she's never noticed it before. She often walks along this street, and since she always manages to see the camp from her house, she knows there are not many other people walking there. "What is that?" she says to herself as the glow becomes brighter. She looks questioningly at her house, hoping to get at least a small clue to her question. In a blink of an eye, she shakes her head and gets to the bottom of the matter. Slowly she approaches the glow and also imagines hearing a slight rattle. After a few steps, Marie arrives and is amazed when she realizes that it is a completely normal stone. Just a stone that shines. But why does it shine? The girl crouches down and reaches the stone. As soon as she touches it, q feeling of calm and relaxation flows into her body. She smiles and looks carefully at the piece from all sides. Shortly afterward he puts it in his jacket pocket, to take it home with him. Marie realizes that suddenly she is much happier and the best thing is that she has just come up with an idea for her essay. He decides not to tell a holiday or a story of his life, but a fantastic adventure. Marie loves to invent stories and put them on paper, and she feels that this stone would help her write her essay and present it with flying colors. While not touching it, and despite its tiny size, almost not to be noticed in her pocket, she feels that it is close to her. Marie's doubts fade a little more with each step. She runs the last few meters to her house because she wants to start the essay as soon as possible. Through the garden, she rushes to the front, opens the door, and enters the house. "I'm back," she shouts to her family as she takes off her shoes. They are all sitting comfortably in the living room watching a movie. They do this often when the weather is not so good on Sundays. Her family consists of her two younger brothers, her mother, and her father. "We're watching a movie, do you want to join us?" her father asks her from the hallway. "You still have time to come to understand the story, because it's just starting." Marie shows herself very briefly at the door of the living room. She smiles and shakes her head. "No, maybe later," she replies, pointing upwards in the direction of her room. "I want to start the essay because I just came up with an idea." Everyone nods and returns her smile. Not even a breath later, Marie turns around, takes the stone from the bag, and hangs her jacket on the coat rack. Then she hurries up the stairs and disappears into her room. She wastes no time: she takes a notebook and a pen and sits at his desk. She puts the stone, which has now lost its splendor, next to her table lamp. As she is sitting at her desk, she has unlimited views of the field and the forest. Marie has always been very enchanted by this little piece of forest. She has been walking there several times with her parents and brothers, it was just a normal forest, but she always imagined that she was enchanted and that unicorns lived there. And it is precise of these unicorns that he was going to write in his story. "Let's start," she rejoices and evokes the first word on his blank sheet. She writes about a girl who has always believed in the magic of life. It's no secret and she's fooled by all the people. The more words she puts on paper and the more she writes about the girl, the more she realizes that she is describing herself. Should she have invented a different story? Wasn't that all too obvious? She squeezes her lips and lowers the corners of her mouth and takes a look at her new stone. "Am I doing the right thing?" she asks just like that. As soon as she asked that, her eyes lit up when she noticed that the stone begins to shine again. Then she remembers that with her story she could have made a difference. Her classmates are not very empathetic. If they think that a student is strange or different, they immediately point it out to them and this is not right in Marie's eyes. Everyone has the right to be who they want to be, without fear of what others might think of them. And that's exactly what she wants to convey with her story. Marie doesn't want to change the whole class's mind. It would be a great success for her if she could have two or three companions on her side. "Yes, that's exactly what I'm going to do", she thinks to herself, amazed at this determination, and she hopes so much that her euphoria will last until the end of next week. She keeps on writing: After school, the girl goes for a walk in the forest every day. Marie takes the forest behind her house as a model. One day she meets a unicorn. At first, she is shocked and struggling to believe her eyes, but the familiarity that the unicorn emanates calms her down very quickly. Marie is completely in her element, describing every detail of the forest and about the unicorn, of course without forgetting the girl's feelings and thoughts. As soon as she has finished one sentence, she can already think of the words for the next one. She feels good and is happy. Every minute she spends sitting at her desk, her desire to become a writer intensifies. The unicorn announces to the girl that she is special, so they become best friends and embark on a mission, in which they want to help children who are not taken seriously and are afraid of life. With their actions, they also want to make sure that children do not lose confidence in themselves and magic. When Marie writes the last sentence of her story, she can't believe she wrote an entire essay in a short time. This makes her extremely happy, and now she's sure it would have been a complete success. A small part of her is still full of doubts, but she hopes to convince her in the coming days. And before she knows it, her big day is just around the corner. Unfortunately, she couldn't fully convince herself that it would be okay. As if rooted in the place, she now stood in front of her classroom staring at the children with her eyes wide open, totally excited because all eyes were on her. In the last rows, you can hear mumbling and laughter. Children don't necessarily have to talk or laugh at her, but that's what a person imagines. Someone cares, someone else not so much. Marie, unfortunately, is one of those people who worries and this makes her easily irritable. "So," Mrs. Müller speaks and closes the open window. "You can start now, Marie," he says, nodding at her and sitting in the chair behind her desk. All of a sudden, the class becomes very quiet. So quiet that the silence hurts Marie's ears. She clears her throat and begins to read the first sentence, but at the third word, her voice fails. Panic suddenly spreads in Marie. Her heartbeats and she realizes that she is blushing. She begins to sweat and becomes unstable when a boy in the front row begins to giggle. "Silence," Ms. Müller warns. "Start again," she then directs her words to Marie. The girl then takes a deep breath and thinks of her stone. Without thinking about others, she puts her hand in her pocket and pulls out the stone. Just like the first time, as soon as she touches her it gives her a feeling of peace. Marie holds back a smile when her heartbeat returns to normal and when she realizes she is now ready. She feels her confidence grow with each breath, and she becomes braver. She clears again her throat and proceeds to read the first sentence. And it worked, without stuttering and hesitation. With every word that comes out of her mouth, she realizes that she is becoming even more confident. Holding the stone in her hands all the time, she believes in her history and herself. Marie recites her essay as if she had never done anything else in her life but that. Out of the corner of her eye, she realizes that Frau Müller is listening to her with a proud smile. She then looks at the class and notes with pleasure that all the children are hanging from her lips. This moment is a great event in Marie's life because she slowly realizes that she is making a difference. Not only with the class, but also with herself. The children seem thoughtful, no one interrupts her, giggles, or makes her feel different. Everyone is very quiet and listens to her. For a few days, she has been repeating to herself that she will make it and that everything will be fine, but she did not expect such reactions and such success. Marie now knows that she can do anything in life, no matter how difficult it is. You just have to believe in yourself and your abilities.

It's your turn

What did you like most about this story?

_____

_____

_____

_____

_____

_____

_____

_____

_____

_____

_____

_____

_____

It's your turn

What did you learn from this story?

_____

_____

_____

_____

_____

_____

_____

_____

_____

_____

_____

_____

_____

_____

_____

Olli and the rattlesnake gang

Olli has been standing in front of Müller's kiosk for half an hour. He looks around. They're watching him, he's sure. Who? The big guys call themselves the Rattlesnake Gang, and Olli has the feeling that the snake's rattle is getting louder and louder. What should he have done? Olli has always been shorter than the others. In kindergarten, no one cared, but since he started school, his height had become a problem. Jens is taller than all the children in the class. He had been teasing him since the first day, and he wasn't the only one. When the older boys in the fourth grade felt that his classmates were making fun of him, they joined them. That was the problem. The older boys, some of whom also attend others from the secondary school that is next to the elementary school, did not stop at teasing. The boys of the rattlesnake gang, as they call themselves, had no problem-fighting. Even Olli had already become their victim and was afraid. He certainly didn't want to be hit or pushed, nor to be teased. The rattlesnake gang was ready to stop, but they demanded a high price. Olli should have shown that he had courage. He was supposed to steal from Müller's kiosk. Only then they would leave him alone, but if he hadn't... Olli feels suffocated by fear. Not only the fear of the boys but also stealing scared him just as much. Stealing is wrong, everyone knows it and if he was caught red-handed, he could not have escaped from the police, and then from his parents. How would he explain to them why he was stealing? If he had told them, the big guys would have beaten him. Olli is trapped, from every point of view. Or maybe it would be better to say in a snake pit? Olli continues to squint at the kiosk before looking around again and keeping an eye on the gang members. What should it

58

do? He sits there for a while, ruminating with a hasty look when Silke arrives. "Hey Olli, how are you?" greets him from afar. Quickly approaches. Silke is her older sister's best friend. Both go to high school and will graduate next year. Silke is often at their home, doing their homework together, listening to music, and doing girly things with his sister. Now Silke stands in front of him and looks at him with a questioning air. "What's wrong?" "Nothing, everything is fine," insists Olli. "No, it's not like that, I know you. From the way you look around, something is wrong." "Then Silke," Olli begins, looking beyond. Wasn't there one of the rattlesnake gang behind there? "I can't, you have to go." "Olli! What is it? I see you're afraid of something." "Did something happen? Have you done anything wrong?" "No, don't do it," insists Olli. "Not yet," he adds quietly. "I think we'll go get a hot chocolate first," Silke says, taking Olli by the hand and pulling him with her. "But Silke, please, you don't understand." "It may be, but you're not safe anyway, so let's grab a hot chocolate and talk. Maybe then you'll realize what you want." Olli sighs. She knew that Silke can be very stubborn. And it's true, he's not sure what to do. Maybe hot chocolate would help give him the courage to decide. To steal, or to be beaten. The choice is modest, in reality, Olli does not want either of them, but how could he get out of this mess? Together with Silke, they go to a baker in the square. The kiosk is still visible at the edge of the field of view. Silke buys two chocolates and makes him sit inside. Olli sits down so that he has the door in sight and continues to stealthily look at the kiosk and the other part of the square. "Ok boy, now look at me and not elsewhere." "But Silke..." "No excuses!" she replies while grabbing his hand. "I know you don't like to be called small, but if you don't like it, then you should behave like a big guy." "I don't think that changes anything." "Have you ever tried?" "How can I? I don't know how to behave like a big boy," Olli replies, adding in a low voice: "I'm not a tall guy." "Nonsense, you're as big as you feel you are." "I assure you that if you were not so big, you were going to be teased or pushed but you are a girl so that would never happen to you...". "Oh, that's where the problem is. Is it someone I know?" "No, you don't know them." "A girl?" "No." "Different, then." "Yes," Olli quietly admits. "And if I tell you more, they will beat me." "OK," Silke replies, taking a big sip from her cup. "And why were you standing in front of Müller's kiosk?" "I'm not allowed to tell you." Olli also takes a sip. "They're looking at me," he adds in a whisper. "It's not a big deal. We're drinking hot chocolate, I dragged you with me and they can't hear what we are talking about from out there. But that's okay, I accept it for now. So, you don't know how to behave when you grow up?" "We've already talked about it." "Acting like a great man has nothing to do with height, but it has to do with how you behave." "And what do you do?" Olli is far from convinced by Silke's theory. "First of all, Olli raises his head, shoulders back, and chest out. You immediately seem taller and more determined." "What makes you think?" "Do you remember two years ago when I had an acne problem?" "Yes, right, you looked smaller than normal then, somehow." "That's exactly how

I felt then. Small, abandoned, alone. It seemed to me that everyone was staring at me and when I felt this way, it happened that I was also teased. I just wanted to hide. And then there was this guy who offered me protection if I did certain things. But I didn't want that. I was so scared and didn't know what to do. And then I talked to someone." "How are you talking to me now?" Silke sways her head back and forth. "In the same way. Your sister was there for me, but she couldn't help me. She asked your mother what she could do and then talked to me and gave me a lot of advice." "From my mother, I didn't know either." "Everyone needs help sometimes, but it's not always easy to ask for help. Then it is useful to have friends who notice it and offer help on their own." "This is also one of the pearls of wisdom you learned then." "Yes, because at first, I was very angry with your sister for talking about me with your mother. But I knew right away that it was the best thing that could happen to me at that moment." "So does that mean you're going to tell my mom about me if I don't talk to you now?" "I didn't say that, little man. I said that sometimes it is good to talk to someone. Where do you have your head?" Olli looks at her, at first confused, then feels his head hanging low between his shoulders as if trying to hide in his own body." "Okay, I'll try," he replies while raising his head as much as possible. "And shoulders back, chest out. Up, you can do it," Silke urges. Olli carries his shoulders back and tries to push his chest forward. He takes a deep breath and immediately begins to feel better. "And how does it feel?" asks Silke. "Incredibly good! I never thought it would make a difference," Olli replies with amazement. "Perfect, then let's move on to the next step. When you talk to someone, look them in the eye. As firmly as possible." "You're crazy, I can't look them in the eye, they would beat me right away." Olli is horrified. "Well, I have the experience that most guys are cowards and just pretend to be tough guys. The moment you stop lowering yourself and face them, they no longer have guts." "Okay, then you know other guys like me. I've heard that they beat anyone who doesn't do what they say." "Voices. Have you ever experienced it yourself?" "Yes, Jens, they pushed him so that he fell and he was left with bruises. All this for telling them no. And he's much taller than me." "Did he say no to their faces? He looked them in the eye, head held high, shoulders back, or stood there as you were sitting a few minutes ago, with your head down and full of fear." Olli thought about it for a long time. Silke was right, Jens had lowered his head and looked at the boys only out of the corner of his eye. He had sat even straighter. Perhaps Silke had revealed to him the secret of the greats. "But if..." Olli sank back into himself. "... doesn't it work?", Silke completed the sentence. "Well, you know you don't have to face them alone?" "If I'm a spy, they'll look for me even more, won't they?" "Or they'll get so much into trouble that they'll never treat a child the way they treat you again." "I don't think so. They are not afraid of anything." "Olli, head up, shoulders back, chest out." Olli automatically follows her command and immediately feels the air clear again and feels better. If these kids don't learn now that this is not the way to treat people, they will continue to look for victims." There will always be a little Olli, somewhere, which they will then mistreat. And when they reach a certain age, even punishments will not serve to make them better people." "Are you trying to shift the responsibility for what they do onto me?" "Not really. Realize that what you do or don't do has consequences." "If no one reacts, this will continue. That's what you're telling me." "Yes. So, are you the little Olli now, the one who gets his feet on his head and is too afraid to decide? Or you are the great Olli with his head held high, who knows when he needs help and accepts it." "I am... I am...", sighs Olli. Then he takes a deep breath, closes his eyes, raises his head, even more, carries his shoulders even further back, and then speaks loud and clear: "I am the great Olli and I would be happy if you helped me". "Well, it wasn't that difficult. Now tell me, what were you doing in front of Müller's kiosk?" Olli realizes that he is sinking again and transpires. Then he consciously stretches and looks deeply into Silke's eyes. "They want me to steal chewing gum for them." "Why right in Müller's kiosk?" "I don't know. I just know they insisted that I do it there." "Müller has cameras everywhere. He was often robbed. But, since he has the cameras, he has filmed everyone and reported them to the police." Olli's eyes open wide. "That would mean they want..." "... that you get caught and get into trouble." "Wow, this is even meaner than being beaten," Olli says, trembling with anger. "What wickedness is this?" "Are you going to put up with it?" Silke asks him. "No, I want to fight. Will you help me?" "Of course, I will help you, Olli, we are almost like brother and sister, how often do I hang out with you." "And how do we do it?" "First I have to make a few phone calls and then..." Silke tells Olli about his plan. Then Silke goes to the bathroom. When she comes back, she smiles. "OK Olli, you know what to do. Now I go and you comfortably finish your hot chocolate before going to Müller's kiosk." "Okay," he came out miserably from Olli's mouth. "Ok Silke". This time his words were clear and decisive. Silke leaves while Olli sips his hot chocolate. He looks through the square and in the distance, he thinks he sees someone from the rattlesnake gang. He turns his head towards his hot chocolate and smiles. After a few minutes, he realizes out of the corner of his eye that a couple of guys are approaching. "Are you going to do something today?" Someone asks him. "I hope, for your sake, that you were just talking about chocolate with that beautiful girl," adds a second voice. Olli stands up and turns to them with his head held high. They are three boys from the rattlesnake gang. He doesn't know their names, but he doesn't even care. He simply calls them one, two, and the one who hasn't said anything yet three. "I'm coming, are you in such a hurry for your tires? Why don't you go and get them then?" "Careful, dwarf. Now you go to the guy and steal the tires. And to make sure you don't mess up, the three of us will follow you." Olli knew they were watching him, but the fact that they now wanted to come with him was perfect for the plan Silke had thought with him. "Well, then move, I'm going to

Müller's kiosk now," he replies as he suddenly found the courage. "There was an encourager in chocolate," says number one, trying to look even taller than Olli. "You should try sometimes," he replies. "Hey, don't be brazen," Number Three raises his fist menacingly. Olli leaves the bar and goes to the kiosk. The three boys follow him but keep a short distance. As he arrives at the kiosk, he puts his hand on the handle and takes another deep breath. "I hope everything is ready," he thinks. Then he opens the door. The gentleman looks at him and when the door closes, he nods slightly. Olli takes another deep breath and goes to the chewing gum. The door opens again and the three boys enter. Olli does not look at them, but slowly reaches the chewing gum. "Say, I know you," Müller says out loud in the direction of the boys.

"You belong to that Kevin Wood, don't you?" "Ehm well..." replies one of the boys, presumably the number three, stunned. Olli smiles and takes a piece of chewing gum from the shelf. "What do you care?" asks Number One brazenly. "Quite a bit, because he stole here several times and for some reason, various other thieves say he incited them to steal. Don't you know anything about it?" "They are all lies of little scoundrels like him trying to escape their punishment," smiles Number Two. "Oh, that's it." The miller lowers himself under the table and suddenly a Clack is heard. The number three turns around and tries to open the door. "They locked us in, what is this?" he asks horrified. "This is deprivation of liberty!" says Number Two. "Olli, are these the guys who want to force you to steal?" "Yes, there are three of them and there's also a Kevin, but I don't know his last name." "It is not necessary, it is already known to the police." Through the shop window, they can see several police officers coming toward the store. Number One looks at his companions, stunned. "Shit, the police." He turns to Olli. "There will be repercussions for this!" "Ah, so not only incitement to theft, but also threat of violence, well it's all recorded on video." Müller remains calm. The police knock on the door and then everyone hears the clack again. Two police officers enter the kiosk and Silke follows them. "Wow, three of them," he says, turning to the boys. "Are you okay Olli?" "Yes, thank you," Olli replies. "And thank you also, Mr. Müller." "It's all right, boy, this Kevin Wood has been playing this game with too many guys like you for a long time. Unfortunately, they are always taken alone and the judges then say that it is just an excuse. But now we have three of his gang with footage to testify. Audio included". "Of course," Olli replies and takes a cell phone from his jacket pocket. Silke takes it and presses play. "Be careful, dwarf. Now go to the miller and you will steal chewing gum. And to make sure we don't make mistakes, the three of us will come with you." You can hear the number from your mobile phone quite clearly. "Little dwarf, you deceived us," he shouts as he tries to beat Olli. But a police officer holds him back. Olli approaches the boys with his head held high, his shoulders back, his chest out. "Size has nothing to do with height, but with behavior, and I'm much bigger than all of you put together." Silke gives the police the memory card of the cell phone and Mr. Müller shows them the surveillance tapes. Then the three are taken away. They have to go with them to the police station where their parents would soon come to pick them up. Olli is happy but also worried. The case is not over yet, there are many other guys in the gang, and he does not know how they would react to the fact, or if the rest of the plan would have worked. Silke takes him in her arms. "Don't worry, the rest of the plan will work too." Olli takes a deep breath. "Yes, I believe it. We can do anything if we stay united." The police officers are still taking the statements and then Silke takes Olli home. That night Olli sleeps very well. Somehow, the fears he had had about the gang suddenly seem small and insignificant to him. The next day Olli goes to school normally. He feels much taller than usual. Jens meets him in the schoolyard. "You're crazy, you know what they did to me and I said no." "Yes, you said no, but full of fear and alone. If we all stand together and look them firmly in the eye, we are much stronger than them." "Have you suddenly gotten bigger?" "Yes, because I found my courage. I know there is someone to help me." Other children approach Olli. Some ask him if he feels safe, if he is not afraid, and others say, "It's time to react." "You did the right thing" and again and again "I'm with you." The last sentence is the most important for Olli. "If you're in it, then don't make us wait any longer. Now it's finally time to decide and go straight to them." "Oh God, this is madness, they're going to beat us," Jens complains. Olli takes his hand: "They can't beat us all and together we are much stronger than them. Raise your head, shoulders back and chest out and then look them deeply in the eye and say what we think of them." "Yes, finally, let's go", and that's when Olli realizes that he is not the only one suffering because of this gang. Together they march towards the bushes that separate their elementary school from the middle school and where the rattlesnake gang always gathers. "Ah, here's the little fool," they hear as they get to the bushes. Kevin Wood is already there too. He and the others in the gang who are already there go out to the side of the elementary school. "You have to be looking for trouble. They should realize what happens when they disobey us, and then you also dare to come and scold us?" shouts Kevin out loud across the square. "On the contrary, either you finally leave us alone or you will get into trouble." Olli heads towards Kevin with his head held high. "Oh, and what are you going to do now? Here there are no police officers and no millers. You'll piss in your pants before they arrive. You'll regret not stealing that stupid chewing gum instead of spying on my boys." "I don't think so, because I'm still here too," Jens intrudes, to his great shock. "And I'm helping Olli too." "And so do I"... More and more people raise their heads and unite against them. "You won't think you can challenge us all." "My boys and I will face you all, brats. Let me solve this with Olli alone." "I guess you're too cowardly to challenge us all." "You'll regret it." "I don't think so." "Oh yes, you think so," Olli looked him firmly in the eyes and pointed his finger behind him at the bushes. "A bush is a strange thing. It protects you from being seen, but today it has protected others from being seen by you." "My gentlemen, if you please leave the bushes, you will accompany us to the station", a loud voice resounds from behind the bushes. "Shit, did you set a trap for us?" "Yes, because I'm big and I know when I need help." Kevin tries to escape, but the wall of elementary school students closes around him and he can't get through. And then the police officer came. "Ah Kevin Wood, you are now 15 years old and therefore the age to commit a crime. The judge will be happy." "What? I didn't do anything! Whatever those guys say, they made it up." "How stupid do you think I am?" asks Olli, pulling Silke's cell phone out of his pocket. "This should have been obvious to you." "Well, Kevin Wood, we heard it all. And this also means that we will probably reopen some cases of theft, that is, all those in which you have been appointed as an instigator." The police officers take the rattlesnake gang away and the children, who faced them so bravely together with Olli, burst into ablaze. "Finally free! They can no longer hurt us! It was a fantastic plan!" And Olli also rejoices. He could also be small physically, but in truth, he was already a giant and would never let others mistreat him.

It's your turn

What did you like most about this story?

_____

_____

_____

_____

_____

_____

_____

_____

_____

_____

_____

_____

_____

_____

_____

It's your turn

What did you learn from this story?

_____

_____

_____

_____

_____

_____

_____

_____

_____

_____

_____

_____

_____

_____

_____

Unity is strength

"What do you think is in that forest?" Florian asks his friends as they walk along the bike lane, "why does it scare us so much?" Lina shrugs her shoulders and feels nauseous when she thinks of that dark and disturbing forest. "I don't know," she replies, as she continues to peek through the trees with one eye. She prefers to be on her guard. If she were to discover something that scares her in there, she would be the first to flee. Tim lowers the corners of his mouth and points to the forest. "There's probably nothing in there. We're probably imagining everything, it's just a normal forest," Florian replies, rubbing his forehead. "If it's just a normal forest, what is it that we hear every time we pass in front of it just before it gets dark?" Lina confronts him, stopping in the middle of the path and turning towards the dense trees. A narrow strip of greenery separated them from the mountain. "I'm pretty sure there's something in there," she continues, as Florian and Tim also stop and follow her gaze. "It doesn't have to be something evil, but it still scares me." "In a forest there are animals, and they make noises and sounds," Tim replies. For weeks he had been trying to convince Florian and Lina that they could walk in the forest without danger, and that would save him at least half an hour of walking every time. It's a full hour considering the round trip. But the two of them simply had too much respect for that place. Florian squints and stares into the trees. "I think it's really strange that it's so dark in there, even though it's only noon and the sun is shining high in the sky." He affirms while pointing to the inside with his hand outstretched. "Look. There is not even a ray of sunshine on the ground." Tim rolls his eyes. "It's because the trees are dense. Just take a closer look, the trees are full of leaves," he continues trying to convince his friends to take a walk in the forest. "Imagine if we were now under the treetops, we wouldn't have to walk in this heat and we wouldn't be so sweaty." He remarks on his thought again by sighing loudly and wiping the sweat from his forehead with his arm. Lina shakes her head. "Nothing will let me in there," she replies. "I prefer to run in an open field with 40 degrees then going there." Florian confirms his claim with a loud nod. "I agree with Lina," he says in a firm tone. "There are enough stories about the forest told in the village. We should not challenge it." Tim frowns. "What stories are you talking about?", he wants to know, intrigued. Since Tim has only been living here for a year and a half, he still didn't know all the stories that were circulating. "I've never heard bad things about this forest and I've also seen people walk through it." Florian turns to him and moves a little to the side when they are overtaken by a cyclist. All three greet the elderly gentleman in a friendly way because that's what you should do. "I know that people also go for walks in the forest. I went there to walk with my parents too," he replies, pointing to the inside. "It's not that the forest eats people or hurts anyone, it's just very dark and disturbing. It's known to be." "I'm sure these fairy tales are told to children so they don't walk around alone." Tim thinks for a moment. "If you've been in it before, why don't you want to go with us?" he asks his friend, then looks at Lina, perhaps waiting for her to answer too. "Since you're here in front of me, I don't think anything terrible happened to you." "Well, yes," Florian says. "After all, my parents and uncles were there. They knew what to do if we encountered something scary." Tim finds it hard to believe that there is anything in the forest. For him, it is a normal forest and he is determined to convince even his friends to believe it. Everyone knows that animals live in the forest, and some of them make disturbing noises, especially at night. But they run during the day, not at night. He briefly remembers the last holiday with his parents during which they rented a small cottage in the middle of the forest. During the day the sounds of the forest were not so noticeable. It was bright, it was friendly and there was also a focus on other things around. But when night came, the atmosphere changed abruptly: everything became quieter, and the change was felt in the air. One evening he had to go out with his dog Flipp, and it was already pitch dark. The few small lamps that stood near the driveway did not contribute much to brighten the way. Near the driveway, there was the forest, and Tim was surprised that someone was walking right next to him because on the floor of the forest he heard very strong footsteps. There were noises of creaks and cracks behind, in front of, and next to him. It will certainly be so in this forest, he thinks to himself. He also thinks that now in summer, with these hot temperatures, there are many more animals because they seek shelter from the heat. "Okay," he accepts and decides to try again on the way back. "Shall we move on?" he then says with a smile to his friends. "I'm sure Mr. Becker is already waiting for us." Lina immediately nods and giggles. "I was going to say the same thing." His voice sounds excited and the two boys immediately know why. "At this time, he always feeds the calves. I don't want to miss it for anything in the world." "Yes, and later he also packs eggs for the supermarket." Florian winks at his friends. "I want to help him. It's a great feeling to be able to walk past the eggs when I'm shopping and say that I helped pack them." Tim smiles thinking about the farm jobs. "My favorite thing is to take care of the sheep and the horses," he announces, shrugging his shoulders. "I could even imagine doing it one day when I grow up." The three friends set out to go to the old farm outside the village at least four times a week to help Mr. Becker with household chores. Mr. Becker is a passionate farmer who single-handedly cares for almost one hundred cattle, eighty chickens, ten horses, five cats, two dogs, twenty pigs, and fifteen sheep. A few weeks ago, the class had gone on a trip to Mr. Becker's house to see for themselves how a farm worked. The farmer was happy to have guests who could pass by at any time to help him. "And if you don't want to help, you can just watch," she told him. From that moment on, it was clear to Lina, Tim, and Florian that they would come regularly to help him, also because Mr. Becker had told him that he was all alone on the farm. He would get up every day at half-past four in the morning and would not return home unless they had done at least ten o'clock in the  evening. "It makes me happy," he said with sparkling eyes. "This is my job, my passion, and my life and I love doing it. I love my animals and you have to take care of them." The man had fascinated the children from the beginning and they had learned to appreciate him very much. Lina hoped that one day she could say the same about her work. "But we don't have to go home too late like last time," Lina observes, pulling down the corners of her mouth. Otherwise, I'll get into trouble with my parents again." They don't want me to walk home in the dark." Florian nods. "Yes, I have to be home before it gets dark too." "Me too," Tim says, clapping his hands. "So, let's hurry up." The children smile at each other and continue on their way. They sing a song, laugh, and get distracted, so they don't even notice the creepy forest next to them. Unfortunately, it is located directly between their village and the farm. Before reaching the farm, they have to make a detour through the nearby village, but if they had crossed the forest, they would have saved themselves the trouble every time. But this distraction should have gone well for Lina and Florian as well. "Hello, Mr. Becker," they call the farmer and run together to the farm. Mr. Becker is cleaning his tractor with his dogs always next door. "Hello children," he greets them with his hand. "I was waiting for you." Breathless, they stop in front of the farmer. "It took us a little longer today," Florian replies, while Lina greets the dogs with a loud chuckle. The farmer tilts his head to one side. "Have you taken the detours through the village again?" he asks, smiling because he knows that children do not dare to cross the forest. Tim nods. "We always choose to avoid crossing it, Mr. Becker." "I know," he replies with a wink. "Then put on your rubber boots, so we can get to work." They do not hesitate for a second, they run together in the barn and get themselves ready for work. Oskar the dachshund is always by their side. He is Mr. Becker's oldest and smallest dog, but he is very fond of children, and despite his old age he always plays with them as if he were a young little dog. Before they know it, the children and Mr. Becker are in the middle of their work and having a lot of fun. First, the farmer shows Florian all the eggs that need to be packed. The hens did a good job because Florian suddenly realizes that probably packing the eggs would keep him busy all day. Then Mr. Becker and Lina take Tim to the sheep. Today he has been given the task of cleaning them and putting new litter. After finishing with the sheep, he can do the same with the horses. Tim likes this and appreciates the fact that he doesn't have to do anything he doesn't want. Now it's Lina's turn because the little calves are already anxiously waiting to be fed. She adores those small and sweet animals, and her heart swells every time even simply giving them milk. It makes you very happy that Mr. Becker gives her this task every time. The day flies so fast that the children and the farmer lose track of time. When Oskar barks and watches the sunset, the children realize that they are once again too late. "Oh no, we have to go home," Lina says in an almost desperate tone. "We have to hurry." Mr. Becker looks at his watch. "Yes, you're right, Lina. It's already very late." Not a second later, the children greet the farmer and his animals, announcing their visit again in two days. "We walk quickly through the forest," Tim suggests as they leave the farm through a long, wide driveway. "Otherwise, we won't make it before it gets dark." I don't know," Lina replies, scared. Florian thinks for a moment. "I think you're right, Tim. We should give it a try." Lina is torn and does not know whether to follow the boys. However, she also realizes at once that if she was late again, she probably wouldn't be allowed to help on the farm anymore. "Okay," she agrees in a trembling voice. Florian takes her by the hand, squeezing her slightly. "We'll hurry, okay. We will walk quickly and we will not stop. You will see that we will cross the forest quite quickly." Lina presses the corners of her mouth on her cheeks and looks at Tim, who gives her a nod of hope. "If you are afraid, we will protect you and take care of you." Together they were now walking straight to the forest, and the closer they got, the more uncomfortable Lina felt, because the forest at dusk looks even darker and bleaker. Florian shakes her hand slightly, recognizing the uncertainty in every fibre of his body. He doesn't feel good at the thought of crossing the forest right away, but he didn't let it win him, because now he had to be strong for Lina. Their steps were even faster, and when they almost reach the entrance to the forest, they entered it with courage. Bu taking their first step into the forest, they were frightened by the sound of an eagle owl announcing its arrival with a loud "boo". That's just what we needed, Lina thinks sarcastically. She has eyes everywhere and shakes Florian's hand as Tim runs past them. She admires his courage and believes in his words. She trusts him and Florian and is sure they will protect her. Suddenly Tim stops. "We didn't want to stop," Lina whispers and would have liked to give him a push to get him going again. Tim points forward. "Look." Florian and Lina's eyes widen when they notice a slight haze. "All this is disturbing," comes from Florian. "And at this time of year," Tim replies, suddenly not so sure that his suggestion was a good idea. Florian lets Lina go and takes a step forward. "But now we have to pass by," encourages his friends, even though he has always been one of those who never wanted to cross the forest. "If we go back now, we will get home too late. Come." He extends his hand to Lina, whom she immediately takes. The other hands it to Tim: "Let's not let go, so we won't get lost." And so, the children gathered all their courage by walking together through the dark and disturbing forest. To their amazement, around them everything was completely silent, on the gravel only their light steps could be heard. The fog envelops them completely. Even if everyone is afraid, their silence gives courage and security to the person next to them. "The sky clears further on," says Lina. Then his steps accelerate. The two boys follow her and before they can have any other thoughts about the forest, they go out into the wild. Lina's heart collapses, as Florian and Tim. They all take a deep breath and turn back to the forest. "It wasn't that bad," Lina says in a proud voice. Lina is proud of herself for daring to cross this dark forest without running away in panic. Her friends are proud too. Florian nods. "I don't think I'll do it every day, but in the future, we can try again." Tim is very pleased with their courage in facing the walk through the forest without any obstacles. "We can walk through the forest at lunchtime and make deviations in the evening," he suggests a good compromise. "That's how you do it." The three friends laugh and hug each other. Very happy and proud of each of them, they return home and secretly wait for the next adventurous crossing of the forest.

It's your turn

What did you like most about this story?

_____

_____

_____

_____

_____

_____

_____

_____

_____

_____

_____

_____

_____

It's your turn

What did you learn from this story?

_____

_____

_____

_____

_____

_____

_____

_____

_____

_____

_____

_____

_____

Disclaimer

This book was written to the best of our knowledge and belief. The author is not liable for any damage or loss arising from the contents of this book. The author is also not liable for content that is no longer current. Misprints and incorrect information cannot be completely ruled out. The use and implementation of the information contained in the book is entirely at your own risk. The author cannot assume any legal responsibility or liability for incorrect information and its consequences.

Copyright

Printed in Great Britain
by Amazon

82006680R00047